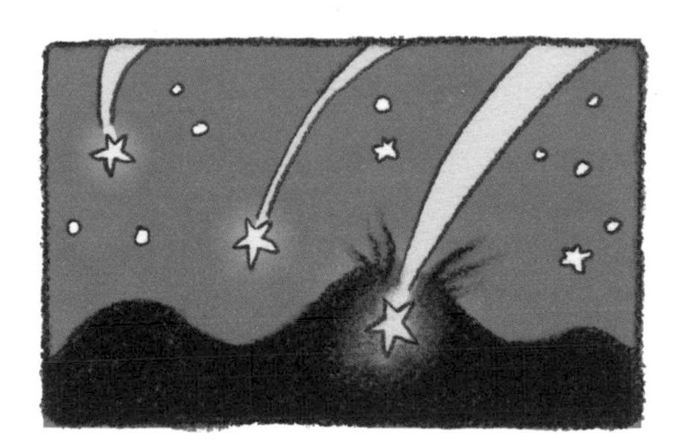

MOVING HOUSE

For Julien and Clio

Published by Roaring Brook Press
Roaring Brook Press is a division of Holtzbrinck Publishing Holdings Limited Partnership
175 Fifth Avenue, New York, New York 10010
mackids.com

Library of Congress Cataloging-in-Publication Data
Siegel, Mark, 1967-
Moving house! / Mark Siegel.— 1st ed.
p. cm.
Summary: When Joey and Chloe and their family are getting ready to move, their house decides it wants to go too.
ISBN 978-1-59643-635-0
[1. Dwellings—Fiction. 2. Moving, Household—Fiction. 3. Home—Fiction.]
I. Title.
PZ7.S5748Mo 2011
[E]—dc22

2010036602

Roaring Brook Press books are available for special promotions and premiums.
For details contact: Director of Special Markets, Holtzbrinck Publishers.

Thank you Siena, Lauren, Tanya, Simon, Jill, Jay, and Sir Jax.

First edition 2011
Printed in June 2011 by South China Printing Co. Ltd.,
Dongguan City, Guangdong Province

1 3 5 7 9 8 6 4 2

MOVING HOUSE

Mark Siegel

Roaring Brook Press
New York

The fog in Foggytown was so thick that people bumped into parking meters.

And streetlamps.

And each other.

"I wish I could see the stars," said Chloe.

"We can see stars at home on our ceiling," said Joey.

"I mean real stars."

"Well, you know it's too foggy for that in Foggytown."

Joey and Chloe lived in the little house
at Number Seven Carriage Street.

"Hello, Home!"
said Joey.

"We're home, Home!"
said Chloe.

"We're moving house," said Daddy.

After dinner Daddy said,
"The fog is just too thick.
We have to get out."

Mama sang "Wish Upon A Star"
and kissed her children goodnight.

"I wish our house could come
with us," Joey and Chloe said
at the same time.

Chloe whispered,
"I'll miss the warm spot
on the kitchen floor
where we drink our
milks every morning."

"And the long
vrooming hallway,"
said Joey.

"And our secret palace
in the sky upstairs."

That night, long after everyone in Foggytown was asleep,

Joey and Chloe's room tilted,

the house wiggled

and jiggled,

and everything went

whoa this way

and **whoa** that way.

"Chloe, are you awake?"

"Uh-huh."

Their house stretched its arms and legs and yawned.

"**Whoa**," said Chloe and Joey.

The house trotted down Old Red Road
and up Bluebonnet Boulevard.
It hopped and skipped at Hamilton.
It did a jig at Jefferson.

"Look, Joey!
Hazel's old home
is falling apart!"

"That's what happens to a house when there is no one to love it. That will happen to me if you leave me," said the house.

"We don't want to leave you!" Joey said.

The house answered,

"I'll miss having you drink your morning milk in the warm spot on my kitchen floor,

and vroom cars in my long hallway,

and play in your secret palace in the sky upstairs.

You've been my favorite family."

“Have you ever seen real stars?” asked Chloe.

“Yes,” the house said, “and it’s time you did, too.

“Hang on tight, little people!”

The house ran and ran, up and up and up, until together—

they POPPED OUT of the fog . . .

"When I was first built," said the house, "the air was like this. You could see the sun shine in the day and the stars twinkle at night. Before the fog, you could see for miles and miles."

“I wish we could come here every day,” Chloe sighed.

From down below the fog, a voice suddenly said,
“Is that Chloe I hear?”

A red schoolhouse leapt out of the fog, shouting "Joey! Chloe!"

"Did you say Chloe and Joey?" asked another voice down below.

"Hello, Library!" their house hollered back.

"Why, just yesterday they borrowed three of my space books!" said the library.

"Why can't we move here?" asked Joey.
"You can, but I'll miss you," said the house.
"Why can't you move here with us?"

A row of gray townhouses quaked in their foundations.

"Preposterous!" sputtered one of them. "Houses should stay where they were built!"

From down below, a butter-colored house butted in: "Any stars up there? I used to love gazing at stars, before the factory."

"Oh, yes! When you could see for miles and miles!" sang a sky-blue house.

"I wish you could all come up the hill," said Joey.

The gray townhouses shivered and shook . . . "But we could get lost in this fog and wander in circles!"

Everyone paused to think about that.

Suddenly Chloe had an idea. “You could light the way!” she shouted to all the streetlamps.

“It would be an honor,” one of them answered with a bow. “Brotherhood of streetlights! Shine away!”

And they lit the way up out of the fog.

It was getting to be
long past bedtime

so the house picked up Joey and Chloe

and tucked them in.

The next morning, Joey and Chloe woke up with a start.

"Mom, Dad, stop packing," said Joey.

"The house is our friend," said Chloe.

"When everyone sleeps it goes **whoa** this way and **whoa** that way!"

"And the other houses—!"

"And then the streetlamps—!"

“Mm-hm,” said Daddy, “that sounds like a sweet dream.”

Just then Mama drew back the curtains . . .

And she could see for miles, and miles,

and miles.